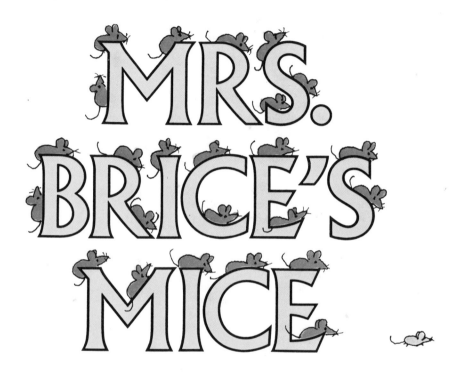

MRS. BRICE'S MICE

Story and Pictures by

Syd Hoff

An Early I Can Read Book®

HARPERCOLLINS PUBLISHERS

This book is a presentation of Newfield Publications, Inc.
Newfield Publications offers book clubs for children from
preschool through high school. For further information
write to: **Newfield Publications, Inc.**, 4343 Equity Drive,
Columbus, Ohio 43228.

Published by arrangement with HarperCollins Publishers.
Newfield Publications is a trademark of Newfield
Publications, Inc. I Can Read Book is a registered
trademark of HarperCollins Publishers.

Mrs. Brice's Mice

Library of Congress Cataloging-in-Publication Data
Hoff, Syd, 1912–
  Mrs. Brice's mice.

  (An Early I can read book)
  Summary: Mrs. Brice has twenty-five mice and they all
do everything together.
  [1. Mice—Fiction] I. Title. II. Series.
PZ7.H672Mhi 1988   [E]   87-45680
ISBN 0-06-022451-7
ISBN 0-06-022452-5 (lib. bdg.)

For D.B.H.,

the one and only

Mrs. Brice had twenty-five mice.

She fed her mice

the finest cheese.

She washed and dried them

behind their ears,

so they were always clean.

Mrs. Brice loved to sing for them.

When she played the piano,

twenty-four little mice

danced around her.

One very small mouse

danced on top of her hand.

He was afraid to fall

between the keys.

9

When Mrs. Brice went to bed,

twelve little mice

slept on one side of her.

Twelve little mice

slept on the other side.

One very small mouse

slept on the clock,

in case he wanted to know

what time it was.

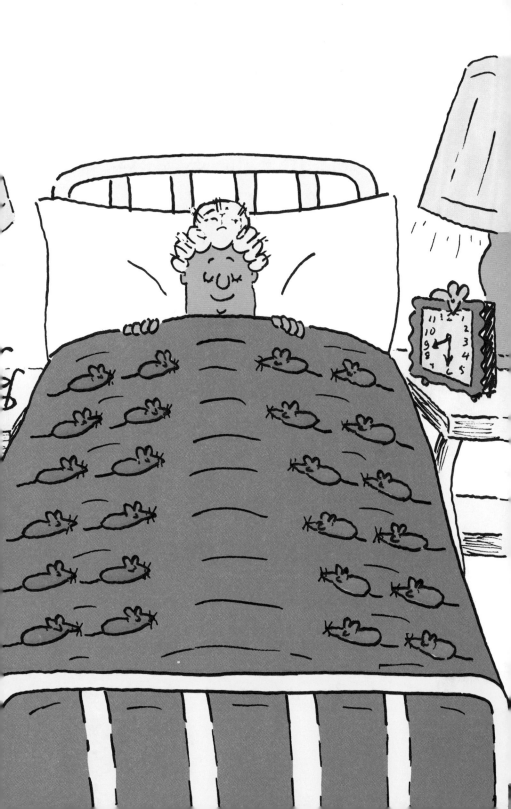

In the morning,

Mrs. Brice did exercises.

She stretched

her arms and legs.

She bent over

and touched her toes

with her fingers.

12

"One, two, three,

four, five, six....

One, two, three,

four, five, six...."

Twenty-four little mice

did exercises too.

They stretched,

they bent,

14

they touched their toes.

One very small mouse

kept on sleeping.

"It is time for our walk,"
said Mrs. Brice.

Twelve little mice

walked in front of her.

Twelve little mice

walked in back.

One very small mouse

sat on top

of Mrs. Brice's hat,

so he could see

where they were going.

He saw a cat.

Twelve little mice

ran this way.

Twelve little mice

ran that way.

One very small mouse

jumped down to the ground

and ran this way and that.

He ran so many different ways,

the cat got tired of chasing him

and went back

to whatever he had been doing.

"What a clever little mouse
you are," said Mrs. Brice.
"Now we can go
to buy some food."

21

Twenty-four little mice

sat in a cart

and enjoyed the ride.

One very small mouse

sat in front.

They went up one aisle.

They went down another.

Mrs. Brice bought

food in cans,

food in jars,

cold food,

hot food.

25

"Now we can go home,"

said Mrs. Brice.

Twenty-four little mice

were glad.

But one very small mouse

kept on leading the way.

He led them

to the dairy counter.

Mrs. Brice bought

a nice, big cheese.

28

Then she and her mice
went home to eat it.

After they ate,

Mrs. Brice sang

and played the piano.

Twenty-four mice

danced around her.

31

One very small mouse

kept right on eating.

The

End